Body Count

A Caution Tape Short

JD Midnight

Copyright © 2024 by [JD Midnight and Molly Doyle]

All rights reserved.

Edited by The Havoc Archives

Cover art by designsbycharlyy

No portion of this book may be reproduced in any form without written permission from the publisher or author, except as permitted by U.S. copyright law.

Content Warning

This a story of graphic violence and extreme sexual content. If you are not 18+ or are not comfortable with such content, please disengage with this content at once. **Trigger warnings include** (but are not limited to): degradation, spitting, oral sex, humiliation, coercion, grave defiling, violence, biting, etc.

Please keep in mind that these characters are an extreme hyperbole; they in no way reflect reality. They are horror movie villains put to page who's only function is to shock and entertain. The contents of this book in no way reflect real life views of the author.

Contents

Introduction	1
1. Body Count	5
2. 27 Minutes	31
Acknowledgements	45
About the Author	47

Introduction

What follows are two short stories.

The first features Cora and Nolan, characters from Caution Tape written with my co-author Molly Doyle. This story is not to be considered canon — it is an offshoot. While elements of the scenes may be included in the sequel, there is no guarantee.

Body Count is for the sickos who want Halloween Stores to be year-round.

The events of this story happen after Caution Tape. In that book, a burgeoning serial killer, Nolan, meets a young woman who echoes his particular bloodthirst. Together, they engage in an escalating game of sex and blood that ultimately ends in Cora fleeing town.

This story picks up months, maybe years, later. Nolan has been hunting her for a long time.

Nolan and Cora are enemies. Well, enemies *AND* lovers at the same time. They have a sordid history you can read all about in Caution Tape. But if you're new to these monsters, all you need to know is this:

Nolan is a serial killer. A seething sociopath who doesn't fully believe other people are real; they are playthings to him, meat to be toyed with and discarded.

Cora is...

Well, Cora might be worse.

The second, 27 Minutes is a romantic short story that is in no way connected to Caution Tape. A palette cleanser, so to speak. I am releasing this small book on Valentine's Day, 2024 and thought having two drastically different love stories from one writer would be interesting. 27 Minutes is a much more literary story that plays with idea of being set in your ways and the friction another person causes when they attempt to join your life.

There are no trigger warnings I can think of for that story; just be warned that if you're here for the blood and the chaos, you're in for some whiplash after Body Count.

I hope you enjoy both stories, but most of all, thanks for reading.

-JD Midnight

Body Count

Nolan

I like being a stalker. You don't have to think. Pick a target and follow in their wake. They move, you move. You're a cobra hunting in high grass, except you're in a stolen car parked on a dark street in some copy-printed American city.

It feels good to be back in the cool darkness, coiled and waiting to unleash all my rage.

Oh, Cora. I've traveled a very long way to get my hands on you again.

That image of myself returns. The road virus. My mouth unhinged like a snake, swallowing the road at a dizzying gulp as I speed along, the yellow divider line getting slurped like a spaghetti noodle as trees, houses, and towns blur by me.

I want to devour this place.

And I'll start with her; the annoying meat stuck in my teeth.

I have to rip her out and swallow her.

The door opens to the dingy apartment building and my pulse stutters. It's the first time I've seen Cora in a long time, since she left me bleeding. The knife wound in my side twinges as if it senses its master.

She descends the steps, wearing black boots and a shiny black skirt with a leather jacket. Her hair is done up in a bun.

A man leaves the apartment, too. In the faint light of the street lamps, I can see that he is large and broad shouldered. He places a hand on Cora's back and guides her down the stairs.

I'll rip out his fingernails and jam them between his teeth.

They descend the steps and get into a car. The headlights click on and it slowly drives away. I wait a few moments, and then turn my own car on.

I follow at a distance, careful to let a few cars between us. They drive away from the city lights, the landscape thinning into scraggly wheat fields and hilly wooded areas. We pass grain silos and cattle farms, less and less civilization dotting the horizon.

I stay back, maybe half a mile. I'm risking losing them but I'll give myself away if I get too close. My fingers drum on the steering wheel. I'm giddy.

"Are you excited to see her or excited to kill her?" Natalie asks. She appears in the passenger seat. I look over, expecting her rotting corpse routine. Instead, she's dressed like Cora. The skirt rides up her thighs. She catches me looking, smirks, and begins to put her hair up. I've been having visions of my dead ex-girlfriend ever since Cora and I killed her together. Sometimes, she's nothing but a skeleton in young women's clothing, cackling at me from passing cars or sitting in a chair next to my bed and watching me. But lately she's been getting more and more verbose, as though my brain enjoys the exercise of giving her dialogue. My private corpse puppet. My cadaver ventriloquist doll.

I look away, trying to focus on the road. "Come on, Nolan," a different voice says.

I look back at Natalie, except now she is Cora.

"Don't you miss me?" she asks.

I close my eyes and open them again. They're gone. I've never met anyone with hallucinations and I don't particularly care to. But if I did, I'd ask if they ever wanted to fuck them. If it was possible. Just once.

Red brake lights flare in front of me. They're slowing down to turn.

They end up pulling off the main road and cutting down a dirt path. I tap my brakes, slowing my car until they've turned fully out of sight before racing to catch up, whipping the steering wheel to the left. The car jostles as the tires leave smooth pavement and are greeted with uneven dirt and gravel. I trundle along, humming.

Maybe she's luring him here to kill him.

"You'd like that, huh?" Cora says. I look down, and her head is resting on my right thigh, her face aimed at me as she smiles wickedly. "You just love it when I'm bad, don't you?"

I ignore her.

"Oh, Nolan, pay attention to me." Out of the corner of my eye, I see her hands slipping down the front of her body. She catches the edge of her skirt and lifts it. Her bare legs kick back and forth slowly, daring me to look.

I've lost the car I'm trailing. It's risky, but I accelerate. The car growls, kicking dust and dirt as it climbs a brief hill. I turn on the brights. Wide beams of light cut through the darkness, illuminating silent but judgmental trees that watch from either side of the road.

"I know I make you nervous," Cora says. "All you've done is think about me the *entiiire* time I've been gone."

Where the fuck did this car go?

"Do you think about me, killing ?"

They can't have gotten far. Maybe I missed a road.

"Do you think about me, fucking?"

My hands grip the steering wheel tighter.

"Sometimes I don't wear panties when I kill someone. It feels extra naughty, you know?"

I look down at her—furious, aroused, frustrated. But, of course, she's gone. All I can see is my erection, throbbing painfully against the fabric of my pants.

I love being mentally ill. It's not inconvenient at all.

The headlights catch a sign. It's the only thing that makes sense. Trenton Cemetery. An arrow points left, down a road that is even worse than this one. I turn down it, and very quickly the wrought iron fence of the cemetery comes into view. I pull the car over and turn it off. I take my gloves out of the glovebox and put them on, stretching my fingers to fill the gaps, relishing their texture against my skin.

"What are you going to say to her?" Natalie asks.

"Shut up." I get out of the car. There's a slight chill in the air, a brisk wind cutting through the cemetery, ruffling the grass and making the trees whisper. I look around, enjoying the fresh air before moving to my trunk.

Cora is there, leaning against it. I do a double take, making sure it is just my own goddamn mind taunting me.

"You'd better tell me you missed me." She pouts, crossing her arms.

"Wanna know how I know you're a hallucination?" I ask her. "The real Cora would've stabbed me by now."

She vanishes when I walk through her and pop the trunk open. I grab the tire iron, a hefty L of metal. I twirl it in my hands and imagine the man who touched Cora choking on it as I shove it down his throat.

Natalie glides around the car like a vindictive ghost. "Imagine how it'd feel to shove your cock down Cora's throat until she apologizes."

If they don't shut up, my next victim will be myself.

The fence is ornamental and old. In several spots, the bars are bent or broken enough for me to slip through. The cemetery is pitch black as I creep along, attracted like a moth to the only thing I can see, two dim white lights in the distance. Muffled voices murmur back and forth.

I'm shadow and ink as I slip between headstones, gravestones, and tombstones. I keep an eye on those lights but always manage to put something between us—a tree, a low hill, a Civil War statue. My eyes are adjusting to the darkness as I draw closer. I can see their outlines as the lights bounce between them. I hear a shovel scraping dirt. A man snaps, "Hold the damn light still."

They have their backs to me as I slink low, drawing even with a hill and laying prone, my arms damp from the dew on the grass. I crawl to the crest of the hill and watch.

They're digging a grave.

Well, digging into a grave. It's a fresh one; the dirt is a solid lump beside a lone headstone. No grass or weeds have bothered to grow yet.

There's a body wrapped in a tarp resting at their feet as Cora aims the flashlight and the man leans in and shoves the shovel blade into the earth. He grunts and scoops some out. She tells him to hurry up.

"I look good, don't I?" Cora—my Cora—remarks. She's laying next to me now, looking up at the stars, as though we were at a picnic. "I must've moved on. That must be my new boyfriend." She smiles slyly. "He's taller than you."

"Shut. The. Fuck. Up."

"His arms are thicker, too. I wonder if his penis is bigger—"

I reach out to grab her throat but she's gone. I hear her laughing in the distance, but quickly figure out that it's real Cora, laughing at the guy with the shovel.

After a while, the man steps down into the hole he's created. "Hand me the body," he says.

"Hang on," Cora replies. "Open the coffin."

"Why?"

"If we bury a body like this a dog will smell it. We put it in a coffin with another corpse, it's less likely to be found."

She's smart. It's a good idea.

The man groans. "You open it, then."

She fixes her hair and steps aside while he climbs out of the grave. A moment later, I hear wood crack as Cora does something with the shovel.

They still don't see me.

Gripping the tire iron, I descend the hill, crouch-running past graves until I'm directly behind this big, stupid fucker as he leers over Cora. I swing low, the tire iron humming through the air until it collides with a sickening force against the back of his ankle. His screams are enchanting. Delightful in the cool night. His leg sags and he drops to one knee.

That's right, kneel for me.

His eyes are wide, bright and dumb. His face is an oval, and there's a surge of satisfaction when I realize he's balding in the front. The heavy end of the tire iron caves his skull in. A monstrous vibration jolts through my hand, the iron wobbling violently.

Give him credit, though. The big doofus tries to stand. His mouth is full of blood and loose teeth—he must've clenched his jaw when I hit him in the head. He spits out a bunch of chunky, reddish soup and fumbles with something, pulling it out of his belt.

A knife.

He swings it lazily at me, one eye casting around in wild desperation, the other one blood-filled and glassed over. "Wuh," he croaks. I know I'm going to repeat "wuh" to myself, cackling for weeks.

I take the knife from him gently. It's long, serrated, and very sharp. I like it a lot.

To my left, Cora is silent. I can feel her eyes on me. She watches as I tilt the man's head back, his mouth falling open by natural reaction, and jam the tire iron into it, scraping the back of his throat and causing him to retch. His arms flail, swinging at me, before both hands wrap around the iron and try to pull it out. I place one boot on his chest and pin him to the ground, leaning my full weight down. He gurgles for a moment, sputtering like a sprinkler with low water pressure, then falls quiet.

Cora's still in the hole with an open casket behind her. I scoop up the discarded flashlight and aim it at her. She squints and steps aside, revealing a corpse that doesn't have a head. It's dressed in a suit, but I can tell it's missing significant portions of itself. It lays flat in some spots, like loose puzzle pieces you sort out, knowing vaguely they belong to the same area of the puzzle but not able to fit them together yet.

"You didn't have to do that," she says, nodding at the freshly dead man at my feet.

"Yeah, I seem to keep killing the men in your life."

"Well, I know how to pick them," she remarks, glaring at me. Her eyes slide from side to side, plotting an escape. I reach down and retrieve my tire iron from her boyfriend's throat, and step to the edge of the grave.

"One of yours?" I ask, pointing the bloody iron at the coffin.

"Yep. Chainsaw. They never found all the parts."

"Impressive."

"Yeah, my ex-boyfriend taught me a lot."

"He sounds charming. Did it end well?"

Oh, man. Those eyes. Like she wants to peel my skin off and choke me with it.

"He was a liar. It was a very toxic relationship, you know how it goes."

"Yeah, I had something similar happen. Girl was crazy. Left me with a nasty scar."

"Was she crazy or did you piss her off?"

I kneel so our faces are nearly touching. The tire iron hangs loosely in my hands, dripping into the hole. "That's something a crazy girl would say."

"You're the one who drove thousands of miles just to see me."

"I've been watching the news. You've been taking jawbones. That's my thing."

She leans her elbows on the edge of the grave, cocking her head to the side, a loose strand of dark hair falling over her eyes. "Is the big bad serial killer mad that a little girl is taking his shine? Are you upset I have more kills than you? Most guys want to know how many people I've slept with. You just want to know how many I've killed." Cora purses her lips and kisses the tip of the tire iron, a smear of blackish blood imprinting on her lips. "I'm smarter than you, Nolan. I'm quicker, nastier, better. You can do your Dexter Morgan, Patrick Bateman schtick all you want, but when they're writing the blood-soaked pages of us, I'll be the one they remember." She takes the head of the tire iron between her teeth, her mouth stretching around it while she widens her eyes to look at me with innocent adoration. "I'm the female killer who played how the boys do. And I did it better than all of you."

Jesus Christ.

"You don't have more kills. I have all the ones from back home—"

She licks the blood from her lips. "Oh, no baby, remember? They blamed me for that." Her grin seems to unhinge from her face, disconnected entirely from the fury in her eyes. "So kill me or fuck me, but most importantly, get out of my way."

That's it. I love this woman. Wherever she goes, I want to go. Whatever blood she wants to spill, I'll hand her the knife.

The thought is brief, searing and alarming. I stop myself from saying it. Self-preservation protocols step in—the old mechanisms of cold unfeeling unsure of how to handle hot, aching emotion.

Run.

That's a brilliant idea, I'll do that.

Like a tortured ghost lunging out of hell, she seizes the front of my shirt and pulls. I can't react in time, my weight sending me careening into the grave with her. Cora is pinned underneath me, with my hand on a dead arm and my face underneath Cora's chin, her arms slipping around my waist and holding me tightly.

No woman should smell this fucking good.

Maybe it's the formaldehyde, the cemetery dirt, the fresh coppery smell of blood or the death, rot, and decay mixed with Cora's light perfume, but it fuses together and smells almost like bubblegum.

I would stay in this grave forever.

Beneath me, Cora scoots backwards, stretching out in the coffin, the wood creaking and groaning with our combined weight. The corpse pieces shift and move, displaced by our motion. A gray hand that's missing fingernails is above Cora's head. My knee is going into something soft that isn't her... Maybe a torso? A thigh?

Cora's hand slithers into my pants, her nails grazing that sensitive, ticklish spot just above my cock. She grips me like she owns me—she does, fuck it, right now she does—and whispers, "I'll tell you how I killed them if you fuck me rotten in this coffin."

I'm in love! *Love!*

I can't get her fucking jacket off; it's pinned beneath her, but I manage to peel some of it off her shoulders so I can kiss her collar bone, nibbling on it with fierce, urgent bites. There's no room in this coffin for all I want to do. It's driving me insane. My hands can't seem to find enough of her bare skin to touch. I'm fumbling, clumsy, like a teenager touching a girl for the first time.

The edge of her underwear rubs against the side of my cock as she takes me and shoves me into her. She isn't gentle, she isn't patient. She knows exactly what she wants and I can only be glad that what she wants is me.

Her pussy feels so good, I want to crush her trachea. I'm angry at how my body craves her, outraged at the way my spine tingles when her breath graces my ear. That tiny gasp from her when I slide in fully makes me stop and breathe deeply through my nose so I don't come immediately. Her underwear cuts abrasively against my cock as I start to fuck her, the friction hot, fierce, and maddening.

"The first one… the first one I did without you," Cora mumbles in my ear. Her fingers clutch the back of my head, using my hair like handrails, our bodies thudding against the wooden walls of the coffin. "It was a married man. I did the same thing you did. Used an app. Didn't show my face, fuck—" She pauses as I raise myself onto my knees slightly, my cock hitting her at a new angle. "We went to a boardwalk. By a river. There was no one around."

I groan. I can picture the cold, black water. The sound of water slapping against the seawall below them as they walked.

The same sound Cora's pussy makes when I fuck her.

"I pushed him in." She moans, and I punch the side of the coffin to keep from coming. The pain radiates up my arm but it works.

"Keep going, Cora. Tell me how rotten you are."

Her nails dig into my throat as she turns her demonic little face to me, rocking with the motion of me. "I can feel you getting harder."

My teeth grit together. I really can't handle her eyes. "Tell me what you did."

"I pushed him in. He was a good swimmer. But I walked alongside him as he swam." Now her teeth are gritted as she shakes her head back and forth, raising her arms, knocking away the dead hand beside her.

I don't know if she's orgasming because of me or because of the murder she committed.

"He would get to shore—oh, God keep doing that, don't stop—he kept swimming to shore and I would kick him, I'd kick him in the face—"

I laugh. I can't help it. She's pure evil.

Her breath hitches and she struggles to form the words. "He slipped beneath the water. I can't stop thinking about it. I—"

I sit up and flip her left leg over, turning her hips sideways, while leaning in to kiss those pretty, bloody lips. She tastes of copper, coffee, and whatever sinister chemical oozes in her veins that has me hooked.

I fuck her like—

I fuck her like—

Well... I fuck her like I really, *really* missed her.

She stops talking, her sentences dissolving into grunts of satisfaction while her eyes close and her body falls limp like a corpse.

Are we that far gone, Nolan? Maybe Cora is a bad influence.

I can't hold back much longer. I'm about to force my thumb into her mouth and make her look me in the eyes while I come inside her when she springs back to life, that demonic glint in her eyes again. A knife arcs from my left. It's that stupid knife her boyfriend had. I must've dropped it into the coffin. It whistles as she attempts to bury it in the side of my face. I lean back, my dick straining against the inside of her pussy. The blade clips the tip of my nose, drawing blood.

Snarling, I grab Cora's wrist and twist it, drawing a yelp from her. The knife falls out of her hand. I grab it just as she draws her legs to her breasts and kicks out, both boots hitting me in the chest. I'm sent backwards into the wall of the grave, dirt tumbling into my eyes.

Cora tries to climb out, but her foot catches on something—a hand? leg? who knows—and she slips. I take the opportunity to shove her back down and her hands bat at me, her teeth bared and eyes livid.

It's like I'm killing a vampire, but instead of a stake to the chest I close the coffin lid on my sweetheart. She instantly starts pounding on the lid. It buckles and rises underneath me, but it's a modern coffin. That means there's a handy latch on the side. Leaning on the lid, I reach over and latch it. It clicks loudly, and it's clear Cora understands immediately.

She screams—oh boy, how she screams! "Let me out let me out let me out! You motherfucker let me out!" I imagine her face turning red. Her fists bruising as she pounds away.

I'm about to pull up my pants and climb out of the grave when the coffin falls silent.

She can't be dead already. The airtight seal was broken when she opened it, and even if it wasn't, she can't have run out of air that fast... right? Then her sly, seductive voice, muffled by the wood, floats out of the coffin.

"Nolaaaan don't you want some more of this pussy?" I lick my lips. I really, *really* wish I had come before she tried to kill me. "You came all this way to see me and you're not even going to fuck my throat?"

Goddamn it.

I see Cora, my hallucination, sitting on the edge of the grave opposite of me, her legs dangling into the hole. "The real me is so hot," she remarks. Right now, I wish I was the type of serial killer who hated women. One of those maligned souls who took their impotent rage out on the world by dicing up pretty girls and couldn't be swayed by dirty talking nightmares with crazy eyes.

Cora, in the coffin, says, "Let me out of here and I'll be your pet. I know how much you like control. Don't you want to wrap me in plastic and fuck me like a piece of meat?"

I jump on the coffin lid, the wood sagging beneath me. Both Coras giggle in unison. But I'm not stupid. I've gotten away with murder; I can handle Cora. Using the knife, I stab into the coffin. The blade gets stuck briefly, but it is well made and unyielding as it splits the wood.

"What are you doing?" Cora asks, alarmed.

"Yeah, what are you doing?" my hallucination echoes.

"I'm cutting a hole in this coffin, Cora. And then I'm going to stick my dick in it. And you're going to suck it like your life depends on it. You know why?" I turn the blade and pry a chunk out. "Because your life does depend on it. Make it good. Make it slutty and I'll think about letting you out." Another chunk comes out. I can see into the coffin now. Something moves inside, and I see a glint of an eye, staring up at me.

"You're going to get a splinter," Coffin Cora growls.

Hallucination Cora laughs. "I love her, she's so funny." She slides onto the coffin with me, straddling and leaning forward to watch me. She's been updated; details from seeing her again applied to my phantom version of Cora. Blood on her lips. Faint frown lines around the corners of her mouth. The new hair carefully recreated.

I widen the hole then reach my gloved fingers inside to break away any pesky splintery bits.

Cora bites my index finger and pulls—her small, even teeth crushing down on the bone. I'm about to rip my hand away when she softens her hold, her teeth finding the tip of the glove and clamping down, pulling it off deftly with her mouth. I hear scuffling as she adjusts her position, then something warm and wet caresses my bare finger.

Her tongue.

Her lips close around it tightly, sliding upward, swallowing as much of it as she can manage until I can see her mouth pressed around the rim of the coffin hole, rough wood imprinting on the skin around her lips, the tip of her nose barely visible.

She lets go, and says, "I'll suck it until my face bleeds, daddy."

What size ring does she wear?

My hands shake as I slip my cock into the hole. The angle is awkward, diagonal. I'd have to lay prone on top of the coffin lid to slide in fully but...

My Cora-lucination is suddenly wearing red lingerie, her black hair in pigtails, thigh high red boots stretching up to the tiniest pair of flimsy red panties. She's on all fours, crawling on the coffin to me. She glows incandescent against the backdrop of night, my mind ignoring any sense of light and darkness to give me my fantasy in pure, pristine distinction.

Coffin-Cora's mouth is eager and enthusiastic. I hear her gag on it as I picture her bracing the sides of the coffin with her hands as she strains to serve me. My hallucination is adoring as she slides forward, leans over the hole and lets a line of drool leak onto my cock. I blink and realize it's my own saliva, filling the role my brain has cast.

There's thudding in the box accompanying the sounds of Cora's wet throat. I listen to it, gazing at my red phantom as she starts playing with herself. Is that her forehead?

Knocking on the roof of the coffin as she sucks me off? The thought is so delightful, so filthy that I want to rip her out of the coffin and fuck her in each and every grave in the cemetery. I want to drag her by the hair from tombstone to tombstone, tear them open and listen to her moan as I make each corpse watch as I defile her in ways that'll send them to hell just for watching.

Cora kisses me again, catching me by surprise because it feels so real and visceral, down to the very taste of her that for a moment, I wonder if she did escape the coffin. But whoever is down there does something lethal with their tongue, pressing it down into my dick hole, the tiniest edge of her tongue slipping inside of it. She tightens her hand around it, pumping her fist with furious strokes, drawing more blood to the tip, making it ever-more sensitive—making it *sing* with agonizing pleasure. My mouth tries out the entire alphabet as I attempt to find a sound to make but I can't. It feels too good—

The Cora in front of me takes the opportunity to seize my throat, turning my head to the side so I can hear her say clearly and coldly, "I own you."

That's fine. Yep, I'm okay with that. No problem.

The demon in the grave makes me orgasm so hard I dig my nails into the coffin lid, ripping the varnish and getting dozens of tiny splinters wedged under my fingernails. I find my voice, but all I can say is, "Fuck, fuck, fuck."

And then it's over.

Cora giggles from the depths beneath me. She might as well be the clown in the storm drain, transforming into delicious nightmares to eat the soul of whoever dares cross her.

My imaginary friend is gone.

I slowly retract from the coffin, trying to catch my breath. I buckle my pants back up, fix my clothes, stretch, and smile around at the night. It occurs to me that there are corpses lying openly in the cemetery.

She'll need my help. We'll have to hide them, bury them. We'll have to leave town; she's for sure on a traffic camera, riding with the guy I tire-ironed to death.

I open the coffin and extend a hand to my dark princess. She regards it warily, which is a little ridiculous considering she tried to stab me.

Come on. Come on, Cora. Take my hand. There is so much blood to play with together.

She grasps my hand and I raise her out of the grave. I help her climb out, and in return, she reaches back and pulls me up. We regard each other for a moment.

Somewhere in the darkness, an owl hoots.

Finally, with a groan as though she regrets it already, she says, "If we're going to do this, you cannot give me any pet names."

"No? Why not, honey-bear?"

"Nolan, I swear to God."

"Pumpkin."

"I will literally kill you. Other girls say that and they're joking. I'm not. I have a résumé."

"I love it when you threaten me."

"You're sick," she replies. But her expression is soft, adoring, and she gives me a smile I'd kill for.

And trust me, I plan to.

27 Minutes

The walk to his house was short, and yet entirely too long–twenty-seven minutes. Too far out of the way for "oh I was just passing by". Any excuse rang false; twenty seven minutes was an intentioned amount of time. If you told someone: "I'll be a few minutes late" in that blasé, casual tone and showed up twenty-seven minutes late, you'd expect a frown; a reprimand.

Perhaps even a scoff.

Twenty-seven minutes meant she was thinking about him. It was unacceptable to be thinking about him as she wrapped her scarf around her neck and buttoned the wool coat and locked the door behind her and started down the steps to the sidewalk. Twenty-seven was an inconvenient allotment; there was no way to be unembarrassed at 9:27 at night; it was such an untidy time. Desperate in its unevenness. Knocking on someone's door at 9:27pm was the same as saying: "I'm incomplete, fix it. Please."

Pathetic.

Twenty-seven minutes was a shameful amount of time for Vicky to walk for this man. It was not the way things were supposed to be; her role was to be aloof, distant. Prim and statuesque, listening to his serenades as he tried in vain to woo her. She was supposed to sit by the window in her apartment while he pivoted and pirouetted about, trying to make her see how they could make this work.

Instead, Lynn (obscene of him, really, to have an effeminate name that felt pleasant to say, ruder still that "Vicky and Lynn" stuck in her head like the catchiest pop song) said nothing. No calls, texts, emails, Facebooks or whatnots. No overtures from this man—she'd suggested, casually (just to test him!) that they no longer see each other. There were a litany of issues, and it just wasn't going to work out.

"I'm not happy." She'd flung it at him several afternoons ago. She expected something, anything; a fight, a grovel, an attempt. He simply apologized and left her alone.

How vindictive.

Bitter November cold–the type of cold that seemed delighted to slash at you with tiny, winter-preview teeth–nipped at her as she crossed her arms in front of her chest and leaned forward against the gusts of sharp wind. She should've worn a hat (no, it did awful things to her hair) and she shouldn't even be out walking the twenty-seven fucking minutes to talk to him, but here she was.

Stupid.

It was so stupid.

It wasn't even going to work out, anyway.

Left-foot then right-foot then left-foot, walking the familiar stretches of sidewalks and brick-bordered cobblestone she'd walked a dozen times. A dozen? A hundred? How many times had she walked to his apartment? Too many, why didn't he walk to her?

He did. You told him it was over.

Didn't matter, this was all very ridiculous. She was going over there to tell him exactly why it wasn't going to work and his mournful dark brown eyes would widen with hurt. Vicky would feel the painful memory forming in his mind, and know she was responsible for it. Then, only then, would they be fair and square.

There was an imbalance in her soul and she meant to settle it. Honestly, there was no reason for her to suffer alone. This was a breakup; the pain had to be mutual and shared.

Twenty-three minutes from his place and she wondered what exactly went wrong.

Well, a million things. A million and a half.

For one, he had no ambition.

Whenever she asked any question that grazed the general, dust-covered area of: "what are you doing with your life", he gave his usual, lackadaisical: "I'll figure it out."

Your car has no air conditioner.

Eh, I'll figure it out when it gets hot.

There's a lightbulb out in your kitchen.

I'll get to it.

Is that job a long term thing or do you plan on…

I'm not sure, I figure... I'll figure it out, eventually.

What are we doing, here, Lynn. Us.

Figuring it out.

She wanted to scream at him. *Figuring it out feels like stasis. Purgatory. A fucking bear trap around my heart, what does "figuring it out" mean? Are you tasting me in your mind, trying to decide if you are okay with tasting that for the rest of your life? Are you replaying every stutter, mispronounced word, failed joke, replaying them over and over seeing if you'll get sick of the sounds I make? I'm a VHS tape, rewind me again, again, again, then play me until I break.*

See, now the thoughts were chasing each other; doubt feeding fear, fear jumping into the wood furnace of panic. That's why it had to end, Vicky and Lynn. This was no good. She was steady; her hands never shook. Her days were orchestrated and precise. Breakfast at seven. Shower. A short walk to the bus stop. At work by nine. The movies on Saturdays; visit her parents via train on Sundays. Her days clipped by evenly and her emotions never flared. Ruthless simplicity that, okay, fine, she could admit, sometimes the simplicity was a little cold. Hollow. Someone in glasses with a clipboard and a sincere gaze could diagnose that as a defense mechanism, so what?

Eighteen minutes.

Am I walking faster?

They'd been having arguments since the second date. He was late, not five minutes late, not ten minutes late, but well over twenty minutes—,

Come to think of it, was it twenty-seven minutes? That would be perfect, if things worked out (which they were not going to) they could get 27 tattooed on each other, instead of wedding rings (but never mind that, it was over, done).

He was late. Trying to be firm, trying to show she wouldn't be taken for granted, Vicky made it known. "I find being late very disrespectful. It makes me feel unimportant."

He nodded, thoughtfully, while chewing on his straw. They were in a "not-too-nice-no-pressure-I'm-not-that-special restaurant" that Vicky had picked out. Of course, she wore an outfit that was "nice-please-compliment-me" but calculated so that when he did compliment her ("Wow, Vick, I knew you were pretty but damn.") she could downplay it ("Oh stop have you seen what my hair is doing?") but secretly be very pleased; with him, with herself, at her own power.

All of that came later, but he was late and that was rude and he didn't say sorry. "Lost track of time," was what he said. "I didn't mean to be rude."

Which highlighted another problem.

Twelve minutes left in the walk. She was a person who never lost track of time. Calendars separated the days with vicious strokes of highlighter pink. Her cellphone had an arsenal of alarms, bells and notifications to alert her to any appointment, routine or errand. Each of their date (he took her to a community garage sale at the high school for the first one, said he knew she liked old books and he worked with the guys doing the floors in the school library, said they were selling tons of 'em cheap, "I don't like books but I can help you carry them") had been circled and rehearsed for. She was an entity of effort; was it too much to ask the same of him?

Lynn operated in a haphazard daze. His life had an improvisational quality to it that she detested. At the end of the first date, she asked, casually, "So... are we going to do this again or...?"

"Yeah, I had fun. I'll let you know."

That was dismissive, and if he had left without saying or doing anything else, it would've been over.

But then he hugged her and that felt,

Well,

It felt really good.

On the third date (ice cream, for some reason he wanted to get ice cream and they froze on a bench next to the scenic river walk with ice cream cones purchased from a liquor store) she talked about her family. Sisters fighting each other, cops called to family reunions. The bad days with her mom. How sometimes she was worried that she'd inhaled all of their radiation, their chemical personalities, and she was chlorine gas to anyone who hung around too long. That she was a bit much, a bit of a lot, actually.

"Yeah, you're a nightmare," he remarked.

"I'm sorry?"

"Don't worry, we'll figure it out."

She analyzed that statement a thousand times in her head. Her only conclusion was that she'd missed some low-frequency sarcasm, because he took on another date after that and brought her flowers a few days later. So, if she was such a nightmare, why continue the cruel pantomime?

Eight minutes.

Fundamentally, Lynn (she was rehearsing her speech) we don't seem to understand each other. I say something and it goes right over your head. When you speak -- and you don't say much–it's like... It's like you're speaking a different form of English that I almost comprehend, but I miss a translation here or there and it's so difficult to figure out what you mean.

Figure it out, figure it out, those fucking words again.

Twenty seven minutes and figuring it out.

Four minutes.

He snapped at her, too. Did she want to be around that? No, of course not. That would only build into actual disdain. The first night she stayed at his house, after... everything, she awoke before him and started cooking and cleaning out of reflex–a holdover from a previous relationship, the sex from the night before activating her like a domestic sleeper agent.

When he found her in the kitchen, fiddling with the broken knob on his stove, he was annoyed.

"You need milk," she said, not looking at him. "And your fridge needs cleaning."

"I don't remember asking you."

"Oh I'm sorry-,"

He glanced around and spotted the pan soaking in soapy water in the sink. It'd been sitting on his counter and looked greasy, so she took care of it. He dove his hands into the water and dug it out, and began emphatically shaking the water off. "Cast iron," he hissed at her.

"I'm sorry I wasn't even thinking-,"

He took her hands away from the stove and ushered her back to the bedroom. "Don't touch my stuff. If I was at your house and started rearranging your kitchen, would you like it?"

Then he took her out to breakfast and laughed at how much sugar she put in her coffee.

Tension seemed to fuel their relationship. They took turns being irritated with each other's mannerisms, baffled at how the other could go about life so completely wrong. She told him he lived like a divorced dad. He replied that she lived like a widowed grandmother.

Two minutes, rounding the corner.

At this point, he had to hate her. All of the gentle chaos of trying to figure it out, and then she ended things so abruptly. She wasn't sure what else to do. What do you do? It feels right, but it's so irritating, it's exciting but horrifying, every feeling the other person arises in you conflicted. Her emotions stacked like Jenga blocks and every time he pulled on one, she winced, expecting it to fall.

His building was in sight. He had the bottom floor unit; his living room light was on. Crixus the Cat lounged in the window, his fat Garfield face squished against the glass.

She reached out and knocked on his door. The wind howled and she shivered on his doorstep. She thought about knocking again, but figured it was too soon. Her speech, like her days, was prepared.

I'm sorry, I know it's terrible to show up like this. I just... I should have been clearer and more upfront with you. I don't want any hard feelings. It's not going to work between us. There's some things that, you know, are deal breakers for me. It's not your fault, you're you, I'm me, it just didn't work. I like you, but, ahhh, those few things!

Twenty-seven embarrassing minutes. An entire speech. An entire list of reasons. All the good sense in the world.

The door opened. He was in blue flannel pajamas. He had a toothbrush in his mouth; toothpaste foamed slightly over his lips. His curly black hair was a tangled nest on his head.

His ears did the thing. The puppy dog raising. He smiled.

Always so fucking glad to see her.

It was ridiculous. She kept saying that to herself all the way into his house and into his bed and into the next morning. She muttered it a few times when they were packing up her stuff to move into his place and after the first few arguments about where her stuff would go, but it was a lot easier than walking twenty-seven minutes to his place for the rest of her life.

Acknowledgements

Big thanks to Havoc and Molly for helping put this together, the incredibly talented cover artist designsbycharlyy, and another thank you to the old lady at the gas station who gave me free coffee the other day.

About the Author

JD is from the rust-coated Midwest where there's more cars than people. Their other works include **Caution Tape w/Molly Doyle**, **Reverie, Reverie, Reverie** and **Black Card Black**, the latter two set for release later this year. For updates, memes and general indecency, they can be found on Instagram @j.d_midnight

Printed in Dunstable, United Kingdom